BEDTIME MOUSE

by Sandol Stoddard

Illustrated by Lynn Munsinger

Houghton Mifflin Company Boston

To Ernie Bel

Library of Congress Cataloging in Publication Data

Stoddard, Sandol.
  Bedtime mouse.
  Summary: At bedtime a child finds that there
are all sorts of wondrous things around the house
and in his very own head.
  [1. Bedtime – Fiction. 2. Stories in rhyme]
I. Munsinger, Lynn. II. Title.
PZ8.3.S8683Be   [E]   81-4078
RNF ISBN 0-395-31609-x   PAP ISBN 0-395-67436-0
                          AACR2

Printed in the United States of America
WOZ 10 9 8 7 6

Did you know
There's a mouse?
Did you know
There's a mouse in your house?

3

Did you know
There's a goose?

Did you know

There's a goose running loose?

Did you know

There's a mouse and a goose and some bees?

Did you know there are bees in your trees?

Well, it's true.

Did you know there's a bear?

Did you know?

Did you know there's a bear in your chair

And a fish in your dish?

Did you know there's a mouse and a goose and some

bees and a fish in your dish and a bear in your chair?

9

What? You don't care!

Well, did you know there's an owl?
Did you know
There's an owl in your towel?

Did you know there's a deer?

A very big deer!

Did you know there's an owl in your towel and a
    deer in your ear?

Did you know there's an elf?

Did you know there's an elf on your shelf and he talks to himself?

Shh! Listen!

You don't hear?

That's because you've got a
   deer in your ear
   and an owl in your towel
   and a fish in your dish
   and a bear in your chair
   and a goose running loose
   and some bees in your trees
   and a mouse in your house

ALL JUMPING UP AND DOWN!

So make them be quiet
And sit very still,

For here is a secret
You won't know until
You look and you see it:

Did you know about sky?

Did you know
There are skies in your eyes?

Did you know
There are moons?
Did you know there are moons in the skies of
    your eyes whenever you shut them?

Did you know
There are faces?
Did you know there are faces and places you've
    seen and surprises
That your eyes are forever keeping
While you are sleeping?

Did you know?
Well, it's true.

And that's where the mouse house is
And the bear's chair.
That's where to look
For the owl's towel
And the running-loose goose
And the big deer's ear
And the fish's dish
And the bees' trees.

That's where the secret elf
Sits on his shelf
Very, very quietly
Talking and singing to himself
About all the things that are true
In the sky full of moons
That's inside your very own head now.

And so,
It's time for bed now.

Goodnight!